Grubby and Skinner

Ron Walters

Published 2019 by arima publishing

www.arimapublishing.com

ISBN 978 1 84549 744 6
© Ron Walters 2019

Typeset in Garamond

Swirl is an imprint of arima publishing.

arima publishing
ASK House, Northgate Avenue
Bury St Edmunds, Suffolk IP32 6BB
t: (+44) 01284 700321
www.arimapublishing.com

Chapter 1

Two twelve year old boys were discussing the building of their bonfire and from where to get the rubbish to build it. The boys' names were Ron and Freddie their nicknames were Grubby and Skinner, these names were the nicknames of their fathers and grandfathers and they have been passed down to the boys and used by their friends, little is known how these names originated. They were so different, Grubby was tall and thin with straight black hair and Skinner was short and chubby with black curly hair. Firstly, they decided to collect the autumn leaves from the streets, they bagged and took the leaves using their old wheel barrow to take the bags to a piece of waste land, which, is the normal spot used on November 5th for the Bonfire. Later that week, they had collected most of the leaves from the streets, they decided to visit the houses and enquire if the house holders would like the leaves clearing from their lawns and drives, and the cost would be two pence. In the beginning, the response was good and they filled the wheel-barrow several times, the bonfire began to take shape.

* * *

They visited the local joinery factory and the man in charge was more than happy for the boys to remove most of his wood shavings and sawdust. Skinner decided to put some of the sawdust in smaller bags, to sell to people for use in their rabbit hutches, or any other animal cages but when they did try this idea, they had very few takers. They reduced the price to 1penny a bag but the house holders were still reluctant to buy.

Grubby decided to take some of the sawdust to his uncle, ready for when he lift his wooden boat back onto the water in the canal. He explained to Skinner that

When the wooden boats are put back in the canal, it would take a while before the dried timber expands in the water. The boat men would sprinkle sawdust on the surface of the water, which, would be sucked into the wooden joints and as it swells, it would make the boat water tight. It's always a problem when a wooden boat had been out of the water and the timber dries out during the winter, while the boat is being repaired and repainted.

"Is this another of your silly jokes Grubby?"

"No Skinner, it is a fact that is what happens, when they put the boats back in the water for the sailing season."

"How about if we bag some sawdust and take them to the boat house?" They did but the sales were disappointing.

They were making inroads into the piles of wood shavings, when Skinner spotted some curved pieces of wood; he went to the rear of the shed to investigate. It was obvious to Skinner that they were curved back legs of dining chairs. Asking about them, it appeared that they couldn't be used because they were full of small shakes and splits.

Skinner went into the factory and found the main office, he knocked on the door and he was invited in and it was the boss sitting at an ornate desk.

"Yes young man, how can I help you?"

Skinner started to tremble; he suddenly became unsure of himself.

"We have cleared most of the shavings and there are several pieces of wood piled at the back, may we take those sir?"

"I'll come down with you and have a look"

Skinner went with the boss, down the stairs to the back yard. He lifted two of the rails and showed them to the boss.

"Yes, you can take them all, as they are not suitable for us to use."

The boss walked away smiling.

The boys piled them on top of the bags of shavings in the wheelbarrow and took them to Skinners shed.

Grubby looked at Skinner, "What are we going to do with these pieces of wood Skinner?"

Skinner looked at him and smiled. "It usually snows in November, we have eight shaped rails, enough to make four sledges and we can either sell, or rent them out. We can make some money."

Grubby burst out laughing and started rubbing his hands with a glint in his eyes.

* * *

Getting paid for collecting the leaves did not bring in the amount of money they hoped for and they were short of the cost of the fireworks they had planned. The small bags of sawdust were reduced to ½ penny but they were still disappointed with the amount they sold. The boys would have no need to worry; the neighbours would normally bring fireworks and brandy snaps, to make it an enjoyable night.

* * *

Grubby suggested collecting old beer bottles, taking them back to the pubs or shops to reclaim the deposit that had been charged, when they were bought.

They went knocking on doors offering to take bottles back for the householder but most didn't want to part with them. A few decided that the boys should take the bottles back for them and share the deposit, they did but this didn't bring much money in.

* * *

Grubby and Skinner were walking home from school, when they saw the local public house getting a delivery. The Draymen were carrying crates of empty beer bottles from the side of the building and putting them on the wagon. Then they rolled several barrels of beer off the wagon, into the beer cellar.

"We have no need to collect the empty beer bottles Grubby, just look at the crates behind the big gates. If we could get some and take them back to the pub we could make quite a bit of money."

"The big gates are always closed and locked."

"We could easily jump over the gates."

"Yes, but wouldn't the landlord guess what we are doing?"

"Not if we were very crafty."

"What! The crafty pair?" They both chuckled.

"Shall we think about that one, it would help us to get some money? We could take them to the small door down the side of the pub called the Jug and Bottle to hand them in and collect the deposit."

* * *

The following day they decided to go ahead with their little venture and they waited until the night of a darts match; there were a lot of people coming and going. They waited around the back of Public House until they heard a lot of excited shouting in the Pub, Grubby jumped over the gate and he passed five empty bottles over the gate to Skinner.

They went to the small door of the Jug and Bottle. They waited until one of the girls came to the bottom of the bar and Skinner took three bottles in and she gave him the nine pence deposit. They watched through the crack of the door until the other girl came down the bar nearest the door, Grubby took the other two bottles in and she paid him six pence.

The two boys ran off laughing ready to share their spoils, they had seven pence each and tossed a coin to decide who should get the other penny.

Grubby won the toss, he got eight pence. "That was easy money Skinner."

* * *

Skinner had just sat down to eat his evening meal when his father walked in, he looked at Skinner.

"The landlord at the pub has told me that you and Grubby have been playing silly devils, you steal the empty beer bottles from the rear of the premises and then take them into the Jug and Bottle and claim the deposit, is this true?" Skinner just nodded his head, "Yes".

His mother just glared at him," Go to your room I don't want a thief sitting at my table."

He got up from the table and went upstairs to his bedroom and lay on his bed. Suddenly, he heard footsteps coming up the stairs, his father put his head around the door. "How much did you make son?" Laughing as he said it.

"Fifteen pence between Grubby and myself."

"The thieving devil, the landlord charged me 21pence to repay the money you had stolen. I hope this is your last venture into theft of any kind?"

"It will be dad, I promise."

"Your music teacher will be here in ten minutes time, get yourself changed and come back downstairs. I hope you are trying hard with these lessons, they are quite expensive and I would remind you, your pocket money depends on your progress." He had a great difficulty in keeping a straight face; he could see much of himself in his son.

They both agreed that their bottle venture was dangerous, so they decided to wait for a month and then practise the words to three Christmas carols ready for the 1st December. Unfortunately, at the first door they started to sing their carols, they encountered several ferocious dogs which came running round from the side of the house. Neither of the boys were very happy with the situation at all. This venture again didn't bring in the money they were hoping to realise. The carol singing was not a profitable proposition and they were both very disappointed. They decided to think of another money idea. Their pocket money was running out, this was mainly due to their liking Chocolate Toffees.

* * *

Waggle Haines and Nobby Wentworth were a little envious how Grubby and Skinner always had money, in spite of them always buying Chocolate Toffees. They decided to follow them around to see where their money was coming from. So, during the school holidays they followed the boys and they soon discovered where their extra cash was coming from. Grubby and Skinner called at several houses on Monday, Wednesday and Friday and collected potato peelings and other cooking or table waste. They then put it in their barrow and took it to the pigsties at the allotments and a man paid them some money.

Nobby said "Right, we can do that and get extra pocket money." The following week they called on the houses, Sunday, Tuesday and Thursday. They had spoken to the local butcher who had pigs on the same allotment. When they took the swill to him, he paid them straight away.

* * *

Monday morning Grubby and Skinner got their barrow out of their shed to make their first call. They knocked on the door, Mrs Brown opened the door. "Good Morning boys, why are you calling today? You collected my waste and swill yesterday." The boys were taken aback. They were disappointed and they quickly realised someone had sneaked into their money making scheme, but it got worse; all of their houses had been visited the day before their planned visit.

"Skinner, we must find out who has taken over our round." As they were walking home, they saw Nobby cleaning out his wheelbarrow. "So that is who it is Grubby."

They walked away, nothing more was said. Skinner went to the farmer's rubbish dump and found two pieces of barbed wire 12 inches in length. "What is that for Skinner?"

"Come round when you have had your tea and I'll show you."

The boys met after tea, Skinner was carrying the two lengths of barbed wire, a hammer and some metal staples. Grubby looked at Skinner but made no comment.

They looked around to ensure no one was about, then they went to where Nobby kept his barrow by a fence. Skinner threaded the wire through and around the spokes of the wheels and then hammered the metal staples over the wire into the fence post. "That will make their barrow immobile for a while."

The boys had just visited their last call, when they saw Nobby and Waggle pushing their wheelbarrow.

Waggle shouted! "That was a dirty trick, putting barbed wire round the spokes of our wheelbarrow."

"What! I know nothing about that, do you Skinner?"

"I haven't the faintest idea what they are talking about."

Off they went, taking the pig swill to Skinner's uncle's pigsty at the allotment. They tipped the swill into an old type copper ready to be cooked for the pigs' supper.

* * *

Skinner and his pals decided to play football in the street; they marked the goalposts on the wall surrounding a house. Of course the ball was repeatedly banging against the wall and Mr Reeves came charging out of his house asking the boys to stop banging the ball against the wall, as it is upsetting his wife. At first the boys took no notice, Mr Reeves came charging out of his house again waving his fists in the air. The boys could see he was furious, they ran off before he attacked one of them. The boys thought he was being unreasonable, okay we will get our own back.

Later that evening, when it was dark, the boys met up by a lamp post and decided to put a fire cracker down the man's drains on the building, front and back. They crept up his garden path, lit the fireworks and threw them down his drains and ran away. The fireworks exploded one after the other and with the drains being small and deep they echoed, making a very loud bang.

Grubby, shouted, "Job done."

The following evening when it was dark, the boys had congregated around their normal lamp post. They were just chatting away when, who should come round the corner, but Mr Reeves. The boys panicked a little, but when the man smiled, they all stood still. They were taken by surprise, they had never seen Mr Reeves smile before and they wondered what next?

"You boys enjoyed your little joke last night, but I was surprised how little you appear to know. When my pals and I were your age, we didn't use Thunderbolts! We would use a jumping cracker, I will tell you how. We would get a piece of twine about eighteen inches long and a long piece of stick, wind the twine around the stick and tie the cracker to the other end. Then light the cracker, drop it down the drain and lay the stick across the drain cover. The stick was long enough, to prevent it falling down the drain through the metal bars covering the drain, supporting the cracker from going into the water. That way' you would get three or four bangs. Having told you this, don't you dare try it out on my drains!"

Chapter 2

The boys were wandering along a lane on a bright summer morning, known locally as the Back Lane, when they saw haymaking equipment being delivered to a local farm. They decided to visit the farm hoping to get a job with haymaking during the school holidays. They went to the farm but when they knocked on the door, the farmer's wife, Mrs Tim's answered it. "May we apply for a job to help with the haymaking?" She turned her head, calling her husband. Mr Tim's came to the door, wiping his chin, obviously he was eating his lunch. "I heard what you said boys, yes, you get here for 6 o'clock tomorrow morning. Okay?" The boys looked at each other startled, "Yes sir, we will be here." The boys went running off, Mrs Tim's looked at her husband. "I doubt if you will see them at that time of the morning but you could do with their help?" They both laughed.

The boys' parents promised to call them early enough to enable them to get to the farm by 6 o'clock the following morning; they too were a little sceptical whether or not the boys would get out of bed at that time of the morning. Both of the boys' parents were surprised when they found the boys up and ready.

They had overlooked, that living next door, Skinner's bed room was in the next room to Grubby's and they had both knocked on the dividing wall to make sure they were awake. Skinner dressed and went next door; he was just going to knock on the back door when Grubby opened it.

* * *

They both ran across the road to the fields and up to the farm, the farmer was surprised but pleased to see the boys. "Right lads, as the bales of hay comes off the machine, I would like you to stand them up, to enable them to dry before we make a hayrick."

"Right sir, we will do exactly as you say." The farmer smiled, thinking to himself, these boys are far too obedient to be true. I wonder if they obey their own parents in this manner. I bet not.

The boys were surprised, when the farmer's wife arrived in the field two hours later, the machinery stopped and they were all given a mug of very strong sweet tea and a large piece of cake. Grubby looked across at Skinner, his face was wreathed in smiles. Ten minutes break had elapsed, the machinery started up again and the boys started lifting the bundles of hay as it came off the haymaking harvester; they were both beginning to tire but they decided to keep going and it was 12.30 before they realised. The farmer shouted to the boys and the man on the machine to follow him and he took them into the dairy, where there was a long wooden table, on which Mrs Tim's was placing plates of sandwiches, home-made bread with crisped, streaky bacon. Grubby was undecided when he looked at the sandwiches but when he had tried one, he was sold; he couldn't stop eating until the plate was clean. He looked at Skinner indicating success with his thumbs up sign. They had the choice of tea, beer or fresh milk. They both chose fresh milk, neither had ever drunk fresh milk before it had been pasteurised, the taste of the cream certainly tickled their taste buds. Their families couldn't understand the boys' excitement but excited they were.

They were going back to the field at night and build their own den using piles of hay, their sisters went with them and Grubby appeared to be keen on a friend of Skinner's sister and he tried to entice her into his den. She refused and the girls built their own den. The following evening they all went up to the field to their den. When the girls went into their den, there was a very loud scream, the boys ran across and they found a dead rat in the girls den. The girls decided to come into Grubby and Skinner's den, Skinner looked at Grubby. "Do you know anything about the rat?" He shook his head laughing, "I've no idea where it came from but they have joined us now."

* * *

The following morning the boys were again up very early and the farmer said "It was good to see them on parade again; it is obvious you weren't tired, we didn't work you hard enough." He walked away laughing but pleased to see the boys again in view of the amount of work to be done. The farmer was right, they both admitted, that they had difficulty getting out of bed this morning and they had aches and pains in all the different places. When Skinner mentioned this to his father, he burst out laughing saying, "You will work the pains off today." He was right, because when they started building hayricks and using the long handled pitch forks it gave them blisters on their hands and pains across their shoulders.

The farmer's wife took pity on them when they went into lunch, she put a bandage round their hands to help, hoping they wouldn't give up. In spite of having sore hands, they certainly gave their full attention to a plate of Belly Pork and vegetables, washed down with ample supplies of sweet tea. Neither of the boys really felt like work after eating the pork and the large piece of freshly baked cake for dessert, Mrs Tim's had given them. As they were walking back out to the field, Grubby sidled up to Skinner saying. "I think we've cracked it mate."

The farmer saw that the boys were having trouble with the pitch forks and gave them the job of lifting the bales of hay off the wagon on to the large pile. The boys felt sure, Mrs Tim's had a word with him. After two hours of lifting and throwing the bales of hay off the wagon, their aches and pains had gone from their shoulders but their backs were troublesome. When he arrived home, Skinners father said, "How are your shoulders son?"

"It's my back now, my shoulders are okay, I'm off to bed". Ten minutes later his mother went upstairs to make sure that he was alright but he was fast asleep, both she and her husband smiled.

* * *

The next morning they were both up early and arrived at the farm on time, they were greeted by the farmer. "Morning boys, I think we will just about wind it all up today and you can have a lie in tomorrow morning. When we finish today I will pay your wages, I feel sure we can agree on a figure, don't you?" He walked away with a smile on his face, he knew he would miss the two boys, he found them to be good company; his wife felt the same, probably because they had no family of their own.

Mrs Tim's brought the tea out at nine o'clock and they were all ready for a drink as the weather had turned warmer. Skinner took his mug of tea from her and waited for a cake or something but nothing was forthcoming, both boys were a little disappointed, she smiled at them. She then, pulled out another bag and produced some warm sausage rolls and they all started laughing. The boys stopped laughing and got stuck into eating the rolls. "We'll miss this Skinner." The farmer came up to them and handed then each an envelope. "Thank you sir." They opened the envelopes, then looked at each other with smiles across their faces. They each had four half crowns; they both said together "10 shillings, great!" To the boys it was a fortune.

Chapter 3

The boys were wandering around when a family went cycling past. The boys looked at each other, that is what we must get, a bicycle. They went to the bicycle shop and looked in the window, where, all the new bikes were displayed. The price tag, immediately told them they couldn't even afford a second hand bicycle.

They decided to knock on neighbours doors and ask if they had any old bicycles or parts to get rid of. They tried ten houses without success, Grubby wanted to give up but Skinner spurred him on. The next house, was exactly what they hoped for. Grubby, knocked on the door.

An elderly, short plump lady opened the door, she was wearing a wrap round overall, with a scarf around her hair and a roller sticking out of the front of the scarf "Yes lads, what can I do for you? Coughing, with a cigarette in her mouth"

"We are looking for any old bicycles, or parts for us to build one, we haven't the money to buy one."

"Come with me." Closing the door, she took the boys into an old shed. A bike was propped up against the wall, it was very rusty but it looked complete. Also, in the corner were a bicycle frame and several wheels and a few other parts, enough to build a second bike.

"Right! You young gentlemen can take all these parts on one condition." Skinner, looked at the lady apprehensively.

"Tidy this shed, I am going to receive a load of small wooden logs and lighting wood later this week. I would like you to help me stack it in the shed when it arrives. I am finding it difficult to lift about these days."

"We can do that for you Mrs," Skinner was trying to contain his excitement. "When are you expecting the delivery of the logs?"

"Will you come next Saturday morning?"

"Please don't let me down, I am unable to do the job myself and I am trying to stock up, for use in my wood burning stove this winter."

"My name is Mrs Anderson, where do you boys live?"

"I live at number 47". Grubby dashed off to get the wheelbarrow while Skinner collected all the bicycle parts together.

Grubby came back and loaded all the parts and the bicycle on the barrow.

Mrs Anderson stood with a smile on her face, as the boys went off pushing the loaded barrow.

The boys went back on the Saturday morning as they had promised and they stacked the small logs in Mrs Anderson's shed as she wanted. "Will you young lads help me with another job?"

"What would you like us to do?"

"I only have a small garden, will you plant seed shallots for me, please?" She went to the back of the shed and came out with a bag of shallots.

The boys dealt with the sowing of the shallots. Their mothers thought they had been very kind but when they discussed how they had sown the shallots, their fathers started to laugh when the boys told them, they had planted them as you would potatoes. Their fathers went back to Mrs. Anderson's house with the boys, Mrs Anderson was surprised to see them again.

* * *

"We have come with the boys, they have planted your seeds, as if they are potatoes." Sam and Albert went down the rows, digging up the shallots and planting them on the surface, covering the roots up with the soil and making sure they were secure. Mrs Anderson, came out of her house and thanked them but pointing out, the boys had been kind and they must learn.

* * *

When the boys got back to Skinners shed, they started separating the parts to make the second bike. The next job was to deal with the rusty working parts of the bike. The links of the chain were rusty and they were not sure how to take the chain off the bike, to deal with it. Skinner shouted, "I have the answer, come with me." Grubby kept asking Skinner, "How"? He didn't answer. They went into the bicycle shop, when a man came to them, Skinner smiled at the man and said, "We need help sir?"

"How can I help you son?"

"My chain is badly rusted and I want to get it off, how do I do it?" He laughed. "Come with me." He took them through to the back of the shop, a man was working on a bike wearing a boiler suit.

"Wilf, these young engineers, want you to show them how to remove a rusty chain off a bike, will you help?"

"Certainly, I won't charge them a lot." Both men started laughing.

He waved them over to his bench, he them showed them how to remove a clip from a link in a chain. He demonstrated how to put the chain back on to the bike and replace the clip. "It is so simple, when you know how, isn't it?"

"How can we get the rust off the chain, it is rusted solid?"

"Take it off the bike and place the chain in a tray of oil and leave it for a day or so."

"Thanks Mister, you have been very kind."

"Not at all," he held his open hand out, Skinner picked up a nut off the bench and put it in his hand. The placed erupted with laughter. The man came in from the showroom." Have you been paid Wilf?"

"Yes," he held his open hand. They all had a good laugh. "I am a little puzzled, which column should I enter Payment, one nut. The accountant will be a little foxed."

"I'll tell you what lads! I will make a bargain with you, you deliver this bicycle to the house just down the road, get them to sign for the delivery and I will put your chain in the oil tray for a few days, or at least until it is ready. Do we have a deal?"

"Yes sir, we will do it now."

"Yes, you take it now, then your part of the bargain is done." They delivered the bike and got a signature. "Job done Grubby."

"That was cheeky but it paid off," Skinner was smiling as he said it.

* * *

They went to their shed, collected the rusty chain and took it to the man in the shop. Looking at it, "Call back in two days, it should be okay by then." They went back to their shed and completed assembling the second bike, this was a beautiful bike. Several days later they collected the chain from the shop, fitted back on the bike as the man had instructed, "Bingo." Both bikes were in working order. They shook hands and hugged each other, success, they were so excited but they had not checked the tyres. Grubby spotted a tin of red paint on the shelf, he took it down. "Shall we paint the frames red? We can call ourselves "The red devils."

"Yes, let us do that"

"Hi Skinner I have been talking to Mr. Meeks, he was off fishing in the River Thames at Bourne End."

"Should we try fishing?"

"We have never tried fishing but we could. We would need rods and reels but they would cost money, which, we haven't got."

"Surely, we can find someone who has fished in the past but is no longer interested."

"My uncle Bert used to fish, I wonder if he still has the tackle, let's go and ask him?"

They set off on their bikes to visit Skinners, Uncle Bert, arriving at Bert's house, Skinner rang the doorbell and his uncle opened the door. "Hello lads, it's nice to see you, do come in, it's great to see that Freddie is with you, I heard that you two had fallen out."

"We are always falling out," said both boys smiling.

They all sat down, "Now young man, whenever you visit me, you want something. What do you want?" Both boys started laughing at Bert's straight talking.

"Do you still go fishing?"

"Ah, so that is why you are here" said he smiling.

"Hi, don't leave my cupboard untidy, if you do, you can leave the rods and other gear here."

"Now young gentlemen, I haven't worked out the amount of money to charge for the tackle yet, I will have to wait and see what your offer is." He said, trying not smile.

"At the moment uncle we have no money but we will pay you weekly as we get our pocket money."

"Now let me see, there are no jobs for you to do at the moment but there might be in the future, I will contact you."

"I will show you how to deal with the rods and reels, there are three rods you may take two and the haversack to carry the spare tackle and of course the floats."

"When I went fishing I always used hemp seed as the bait, boil the hemp, you will find it opens slightly at the side, push the hook sideways into the opening. The floats are self- explanatory, enjoy your fishing."

As the boys were getting ready to leave, Bert showed them how to fix the rods on to the bikes crossbar.

"Incidentally, I will work out how much you owe me?"

"Cheerio you two ruffians", waving them off.

They arrived home, Grubby looked at Skinner," That was a good deal."

Having got the tackle they decided to buy some hemp to go fishing.

The following morning, armed with sandwiches and a bottle of cold tea they set off cycling but they had several stops to pump up one the tyres, eventually they arrived at Bourne End, to fish in the River Thames. They spent the whole day fishing and they caught two fish. They argued about the name of the fish, not sure about their names. Roach was the name for one but the other one, they were not sure but they were happy to have caught a fish.

The time was marching on; they reluctantly packed up the tackle, to cycle home. Their parents did not like them to be out too late on their bicycles. Arriving home, they cleaned the two fish but neither of the boys fancied eating them, they had a strange smell. The neighbour's cat was not at all fussy, it left very little, just some bones.

Skinners mother called them to eat their tea. As Skinner sat down, he jumped up again.

"What is wrong son?"

"I haven't got a proper saddle on my bike, I wrapped some cloth around the metal saddle bar,"

"My bum is very sore". His mother tried not to smile.

Chapter 4

Grubby turned to Skinner. "P C Mathews will be around before we have collected some cherries from the Orchard."

The Orchard ran the whole length of the road where the boys live, hence the name Orchard Road. The two boys intended to collect their share of cherries, now they were ripe and ready for picking.

The boys crossed the road and climbed down into the orchard and they filled their big bag with cherries, it was the biggest bag they could find at home and they hid the bag in the long grass, which surrounded the orchard. Then they opened the top of their shirts, put a tight belt around their waist forming a bag and filled their shirts with cherries.

They were so intent with their mission they failed to see P. C. Mathews approaching. He had spotted the boys; he took each boy by their ear and marched them back to the road. He demanded they opened their shirts and empty their ill-gotten gains into his canvas pannier bag, on the back of his motorcycle. They removed their belts and allowed the cherries to fall into his bag.

"I have warned you two about trespassing in the orchard and what trouble you could be in if you persist in stealing the fruit." PC Mathews mounted his bike and roared off out of sight. They looked at each other and burst out laughing,

They scrambled back into the orchard and picked up the big bag of cherries they had hidden in the grass. That evening, the boys' fathers, Albert and Sam were in the Red Lion having a quiet pint of beer, when PC Mathews walked up to them and handed each a bag of cherries.

"I took these off your lads earlier and warned them about going into the orchard. Will you have a word with them; I would hate it, if I had to take them down to the station?"

* * *

The boys told their parents they were thinking about having an adventure, they were either going to camp by the Double Hedge in the local field, which was about fifteen minutes from home, or go on the river Thames, on a camping punt. Both parents suppressed a smile and told them the camping, would be more exciting. The parents didn't give the Punt a second thought, it just wouldn't happen, they were far too young and it was too dangerous. Having told their parents, the boys decided to go ahead. They took a small tent and a ground sheet up to the field and pitched the tent near the Double Hedge, which is where the parents appeared to approve. The tent was erected and the groundsheet was put in place, everything organised and they went home for their tea.

When they had eaten their tea, their mothers gave them some food to take to the tent with them. May had packed Skinner's favourite sandwiches, which, consisted of a mashed banana, sprinkled with sugar and a bottle of cold tea. Bertha prepared Grubby's sandwiches with honey and a bottle of lemonade.

* * *

The boys went back to the tent just as it was getting dark, they were very excited. Before going to bed they lit a bonfire and sat around the fire as campers would and hung the lamp on the front pole and climbed into their sleeping bags fully clothed. They snuggled down in their sleeping bags, they talked for quite a while, Grubby was still talking and he looked across and saw Skinner was fast asleep. He turned over hoping to get to sleep but he didn't extinguish the lantern, he was just dozing off, when something brushed against the guy ropes of the tent. He got lower in his sleeping bag, hoping, whatever it was brushing against the rope would go away. Skinner woke up with a jolt, he could hear a strange noise, Grubby was half way down his sleeping bag and he climbed up out of his bag, "What is that noise Skinner?" The noise became louder and snuggled closer to each other.

"I don't know what it is but I am frightened."

"So am I Skinner."

"My mother, put the front door key in my food bag, she must have guessed, shall we go home?"

They left the tent and sleeping bags, taking their torches, they started running home and both went into Skinners house. The fire was still alight, Skinner built it up with wood and coal, they both lay down on a rug in front of the fire. They felt safe and warm, they soon went to sleep.

Albert was up early to go to work, he was quite surprised to find the boys fast asleep on the floor. He tip-toed around them not to wake them up, when he took his wife, May, a cup of tea in bed, he told her to be quiet when she got up, the boys are asleep on the floor near the fireplace. She just smiled to herself, so much for their adventure.

* * *

An hour later May was up and dressed, she then prepared breakfast for the boys. When it was ready, she woke them up. "When you have eaten your breakfast Ron, please go have a bath and I will give you clean clothes to put on and put the clothes you are wearing in the laundry basket, you stink of the bonfire."

Bertha walked through the back door," I understand you were invaded last night May, is it anyone I should know?"

"You might recognise the smell of a bonfire."

"Are they going to stay with you?" laughing as she said it. "Albert told me that he found some strangers in front of your fire when he got up this morning."

"When he has eaten, he is going in the bath, he stinks."

"Is my stinker here?"

"Yes they are eating, come in, there they are, "The Adventurers have returned."

"Did you leave your tent and groundsheet there?"

"Yes, we will collect when we smell normal again,"

"That! Will be a long time off." They all ended up laughing. When they collected the tent, they decided that they will have to think of something else to do.

* * *

When they were walking back home with their tent and groundsheet, they could hear a dog whimpering, it was coming from a small shed, they decided to investigate. One of the small sheds had a door open, when they looked in the shed, they saw a beautiful Labrador dog laid down, with a man standing over it wielding a stick which looked like a thin cane. Skinner shouted, "You shouldn't beat a dog like that Mister."

He turned round, "You mind your own business, and the dog should behave." It was obvious that the dog had been badly beaten, they could see wounds and blood had matted on the dog's fur coat.

The boys were really upset, to see an animal being treated in such a way. They felt helpless, they walked back home. When Skinners father arrived home from work, he was told about the condition of the dog. Right son, to stop you worrying, I will go down the road to the visit Harry, the RSPCA man. When Albert told Harry what was worrying his son, he agreed to look into the situation. A group went to the shed, the boys, their fathers and the RSPCA man. When they arrived at the shed, the man was lying down in a drunken state, Harry immediately saw how distressed the dog was but it wagged its tail and went to get up, the man grunted and it lay down again.

Harry asked the man, "How! Has this dog got in such a state?"

"It has nothing to do with you, it is my dog."

"This dog is in a dreadful condition. I am going to take it to a vet."

"You will not touch my dog."

"Get out of this shed, before I give you some of this, raising his fists."

They left the shed and Harry called the police on his radio. A policeman was there in five minutes. They went back into the shed, having forced their way in, the man did his best to stop them entering. Harry picked the dog up, the drunken man lunged at the policeman and the policeman was more than capable of getting his handcuffs on the drunken man. Grubby and Skinner were excited by what was happening.

The man was arrested and brought before a magistrate the following morning, the court was appalled, looking at the photographs the vet showed them. The man was fined and barred from ever keeping any animals in the future. The magistrate wished he had the power, to award the man a custodial sentence. The boys were sure they had done right.

Chapter 5

The two boys were hanging around, wondering what they could do to create some excitement, Grubby suddenly said. "Let us build a four wheel trolley." They both considered building the trolley, with two the wheels at the back fixed but the front two, will have a centre pivot to steer the trolley. The first thing is to find the wheels; off they went to the rubbish tip, "Why is it called the tip?"

"Because rubbish is tipped there." They both giggled.

They started rummaging around on the rubbish tip, a man came out of a shed and shouted. "What are you lads up to?"

"We are looking for four wheels to make a trolley, Mister."

"Come with me," beckoning for the boys to follow him. He disappeared to the back of a shed and he came round pushing a four wheeled pram. "Is this what you are looking for?" The boys said together, "That's great."

The man brought out a spanner and unbolted the springs from the body of the pram. The boys put the body of the pram, back on the pile of rubbish. "When I was your age, I made several of these but we called them a Bogy, if you need any help, come back, I will help you, providing I have the first ride." Smiling, he walked away.

The boys dashed away carrying their spoils very excited, they couldn't decide to which shed they would go to, they knew their fathers would want to get involved, reliving their youth. They had decided on the length of the Bogy, bearing in mind, to save any argument, it would be a two-seater.

There were holes in the long bar which had a wheel each end, they screwed the rear wheels to the plank and front wheels were screwed to a piece of wood, which had a centre bolt to act as a pivot for steering.

* * *

Having completed the Bogy they decided to try it out down the hill at the back of their house. During the second run, they hit a bump and Grubby swayed against Skinner and Skinners left thigh went against the rear revolving wheel making a nasty gash in his thigh. They managed to stop the Bogy and Skinner went indoors, his leg was pouring with blood. His mother wrapped a towel around his leg and phoned for an ambulance. When it arrived, the ambulance man covered the wound and took him off to hospital. A doctor in A&E put two stitches in the wound and the doctor told the nurse how to dress it. "It is a good job it is your thigh, because it will leave a nasty scar." She then told Skinner to keep his trousers down, Grubby started laughing. Skinner yelled out when the injection needle went in. "You said I was a wimp, when I yelled when I had an injection in my bottom. What does it make you?"

* * *

They started work on fixing the bikes, Grubby spotted a can of red paint, on the shelf, and he took it down. "Shall we paint the frames red, the Red Devils?"

"Yes, let's do that."

They started getting the wheels and frame of the second bike together. The inner tubes was still giving them a problem, when they pumped up the two tyres one wouldn't stay inflated, on inspection the tube was perished, it would not hold any pressure at all. Skinner went back to the bicycle shop, as he walked in, the man looked at him. "Not you again, what now, winking at the salesman. What are you wanting to scrounge now?"

"I am looking for a second hand tube, one of our tubes is perished and can you help please?"

"Come with me." He took Skinner into a room where there was pile of old inner tubes. "Show me the wheel and I will sort out some tubes for you. They may need to be repaired". Skinner ran back to his shed and collected the wheel and they both, ran back to the shop. The man rummaged around and gave them five tubes, "Have you a puncture outfit?"

"No."

"I will get you one from the shop." The boys went running back to the shed.

The tyres were very difficult to remove from the rims; Skinner went indoors and came back out with two dessert spoons.

The handles were used to lever the tyres off and again to replace after being repaired. Using the spoons to lever the tyres back over the rims, while doing this, they bent the spoons. Skinner straightened the spoons and returned them to the kitchen without being seen. His mother was very upset to see her collection of solid silver spoons badly bent. "She told Skinner, his father would deal with him when gets home from work."

* * *

Sam was looking out for Albert coming home, as Albert was walking across the lawn, Sam went out to meet him. He caught up with him before he went indoors. "When you have had your tea, I would like to talk to you privately."

"Okay Sam I will give you a shout." Later that evening they met up outside, "What did you want to talk about?"

Sam looked straight at Albert, "As you know, the boys have spent a lot of time trying to remove the rust from their bikes. They are trying to smooth the frames down before they paint them red."

"Sam, they are struggling, when they are in bed, will you help me clean the rust off?"

The following night, when the boys had gone to bed, they both went Albert's shed, the two bikes were there, they got cracking to remove the rust. Firstly scraping and then using a very rough sandpaper, followed by a very fine sandpaper. After two evenings they decided to leave the boys to do the painting. The fathers thought the boys didn't know what they were doing.

When they had gone to bed, the boys pretended, they weren't aware of their fathers help but they were very happy and grateful.

Chapter 6

The boys had both had their 14th birthday and they were thinking of what they would do for a living, or what job should they apply for. Their parents had been in their position, on leaving school and they knew the decision was a difficult one. They tried to help, but children always know best, at least they think they do. Grubby decided to go into wholesale Grocery, with a shop named Lipton's and Skinner applied for an apprenticeship as a Cabinet Maker, in a local furniture factory, called Furniture Industries, later to become known as ERCOL as it was Mr Ercolarni that had started the factory. They were very fortunate as they both got the jobs, they felt sure they would like and progress.

They left school and started in their chosen careers but several weeks later, the whole world turned upside down and War was declared between Great Britain and Germany. Britain was not prepared for war, especially as they had gone ahead with disarming, by ditching a lot of armaments into the sea, whereas, Germany's economy had been built up by producing stocks of armaments. They were quite a formidable foe.

The next time Grubby and Skinner met, they decided to join the Sea Cadets. They both decided to join the Royal Navy, to train as a Telegraphist, if the war carries on to the time, they will be expected to go to war. They went along to the barracks together to enlist in the cadets and they said that they were hoping to become Telegraphists. The man in charge made a note of their request and said a class will be set up.

They went along to the next meeting of the Sea Cadets and to their surprise, six boards, with Morse keys had been set up and an officer sat six of the cadets down. He explained how it was all going to work and each was allocated a call sign. "Now young gentlemen, firstly I have a card for each of you showing the Morse code. This week we will practice the first three letters and next week we will move on to the next three, or if you have grasped those, we can move on to the next ones." They took it in turns going round the room, tapping the keys to send their own call sign, the officer stepped in, to make sure they all did it, using the correct procedure. The boys were very keen and they practised on each other as they were walking around after the meeting.

* * *

Grubby suddenly said "Hi! Skinner. We promised to join the girls at the Youth Club tonight, it is tonight the first night of the dance instruction and we promised we would go, I am going, are you coming with me?" Skinner looked at Grubby, "I'll go with you but this sort of thing is for sissy's, not for the likes of us." They went home to change their shirts into something respectable, Skinner, saw that his uncle had left his jar of hair cream in the bathroom, he put some on his hair and brushed his hair back. When Grubby saw him, he shouted "Coo! Eh, who's used fancy hair cream, it pongs?" They went running off laughing away.

Oddly enough, when they got to the hall they were made very welcome, there were many girls but only five boys, so they were in great demand. The same girl kept getting Grubby to dance with her; he began to think that he must be attractive to the ladies. Grubby appeared to get into the swing of dancing more so than Skinner but never the less, they both enjoyed themselves. They promised to join the dance school in two night's time and they made dates with several of the girls, the twin Burnley girls would have nothing to do with them and ignored them completely. "Never mind Skinner, we will sort them out later". The boys had a disagreement, they both wanted to date the same girl, they argued and it became physical. Grubby went home with a bruised face which would become a black eye and Skinner went home nursing a bleeding nose.

The next morning they were up and went off together laughing away. May and Bertha never fell out over the boys antics. May turned to Bertha "I wish the countries in the world, had the same forgiving nature as the boys. Let us hope they grow up with the same attitude, if they do, they will have a wonderful life."

* * *

The boys went to the next dance instruction, the lady in charge told them that we will be competing against other dance schools in the area the following week. I have been watching you all very carefully and I have decided to match you with your partner. The first names she called out, was Grubby to partner Rose, they had been dancing together quite often, so they were quite happy in each other's company. The lady continued down the list and Skinner began to think his dancing was not up to standard. When she called his name, he thought, I wonder who? Your partner is Mary Burnley, Skinner and Mary looked at each other and burst out laughing. Grubby laughed, the other one of the Burnley twins, great. Grubby was dancing with Rose, the other twin.

Having paired the couples up, she put on the tunes they will be dancing to in the competition, she went around, watching and correcting any faults she saw and Skinner and Mary danced well together

* * *

The night of the competition arrived; the dance hall was completely full of people, mainly parents or family of the dancers. May and Bertha couldn't believe that their ruffians were taking part. The dancers were all called to the stage, their names checked and a numbered card given to them, to be worn by the male partner on his back.

The first dance was a Rumba, there was only four couples taking part. The next dance was a Waltz and the floor was packed. The judges were two ladies and one man, they went around tapping the male partner on the shoulder to leave the floor. Eventually there were six couples on the floor. Grubby and Rose were among the remaining six.

The next dance was a Slow Foxtrot; this again, was disappointing as only seven couples took part.

* * *

The next dance was a Foxtrot, Skinner and Mary took to the floor, again it proved to be a popular dance. Skinner and Mary were one of the six couples to remain on the floor when the music finished, which pleased them very much.

A Quick Step was the next dance and the floor became very crowded, Skinner and Mary decided to go for a cup of tea before the rush at the interval.

The interval finished and the band struck up, there was a long Drum roll and the MC stepped forward. Ladies and Gentlemen, The judges have made their final decision and I will read out the winners.

No award has been made for the Rumba as it was poorly supported but they have been very impressed with the standard of dancing here tonight.

The Waltz was very popular and the selecting the winners was very difficult, however, he read out the winner and Rose and Grubby came second. Grubby looked across at Skinner, making a rude gesture to him.

When the MC got to the Foxtrot, Skinner became conscious of Mary squeezing his hand tightly. They were both delighted when they were awarded second place. Mary put her arms around Skinner and kissed him, he was quite taken aback by her gesture. Skinner looked across at Grubby, returning his rude gesture. They and their mothers were delighted and proud with the results. Bertha said, "Well I never." Several of the dancers were very disappointed not to have qualified for a prize and others who were surprised to achieve a position in the prize listings. The lady in charge of the boys dance school was so excited, her teams had come top of the table. A feather in her cap.

Chapter 7

The boys' parents were surprised but pleased when Grubby and Skinner started attending the local Chapel each Sunday. Some three weeks later, they realised why! The boys' names were added to the list of pupils, going on a free outing to Burnham Beeches. They suddenly became aware, what the crafty young devils were up to, they then understood the boys' enthusiasm to attend. The transport was being supplied by the local vehicle owners. Grubby and Skinner were hoping to go on the open lorry, owned by a man just several houses, from where they lived.

The day before the outing, they set to and whitened their plimsolls, referred to today as (trainers) with a water based liquid, when they dried, they were brilliantly white. The boys were very excited, with the prospect of having a day out for free. Fortunately, the day was bright and sunny on the day of the outing.

On each van or lorry was an adult, whose job was to contain 15 excited children, in order to prevent any misbehaving or any accidents.

On arrival they were taken to a clearing in the trees, where it was planned to have sports competitions. There was to be a Sack Race, Relay Race and 100 yards Race. Grubby and Skinner took part in the Sack Race but they only came third. They didn't manage any placing in the 100 yard race. They entered the Relay Race and they claimed first place, they were so excited. In spite of the boys efforts, the girls came away winning most of the prizes. The girls kept reminding the boys of this on the way home.

* * *

The highlight of the outing, was about to take place. Several yards from sports arena, a long wooden table had been set up with seating forms down each side.

As they sat down, they were given cakes and lemonade, which delighted the boys. One of the boys insisted it was a "bun fight" so that is how it was referred to. It had been a great day, they were all happy but very tired and glad to be on the way home.

* * *

The following morning the boys were still excited but decided to carry on with previous day's plan, apple scrumping. The boys went along the Railway Bank; they were quite safe as the railway lines were fenced off. They intended to go apple scrumping at a house near the footpath. They saw the tree they intended to get their apples from, the trees were laden with red rosy eating apples but first they would have to jump over a fence. Checking they could not be seen from the house, they were hoping they wouldn't be spotted. Skinner was first to climb to the top of the fence and jump down the other side, Grubby followed but as he landed he damaged his ankle and couldn't stand on it, he sat on the floor with tears running down his face. Matters couldn't get any worse, they heard a man shouting at them and a large Alsatian dog came charging up the garden and it stood a few feet away from them growling and baring its teeth. Skinner said "Here boy" holding his hand palm up, his father taught him to always put your palm up, otherwise the dog will think you are going to hit it.

When the man came up to the boys he was amazed, the dog was laid down beside the boys and they were fussing him and he just laid there wagging his tail.

The man was scowling but when he saw Grubby's problem he smiled, "Come along son, let me help you down to the house, have you got the apples you are stealing from me?" Laughing as he said it. They went down to the house, the man's wife bandaged Grubb's ankle and she then gave them some lemonade and biscuits. The man got a paper carrier bag out of a drawer and put their apples in it. "Where, do you live? I will run you home in the car but will you leave my dog here, he seems to have taken to you two."

Bertha was very grateful to the gentleman bringing Grubby home. Later that evening Bertha packed Grubby's ankle with ice and an elastic bandage, the next morning, he was as right as rain (another of Bertha's sayings.) They sampled the apples during the morning and they agreed they were almost worth the trouble.

* * *

They were wondering from where to earn some money, when Skinner's mother called asking them both to go to Mrs Nash's house, just two doors down.

Skinner knocked on Mrs Nash's door, she came to the door and smiled at the boys. "I have a little job for you both, if you would like It.?"

"While you are on school holidays, will you walk my dog each day and if you would like to, you can carry on after you return to school, when you finish for the day, just Monday to Friday."

"I will show you," they walked down the garden to a small shed. "We have converted the shed into a comfortable kennel." She opened the door and they could see an average sized mongrel, which stood wagging its tail. "The door to the shed is locked, I will get you a key cut."

"The payment, we will discuss this after the first week, okay?"

* * *

The first week went well and Pat, as the dog was called, was very well behaved. Mrs Nash called them into her house when they returned one evening. "Now you have completed one week shall we talk money? How does sharing five shillings sound? Both boys smiled and readily agreed. Outside, Grubby did his usual trick, rubbing his hands with a glint in his eyes.

The third week started off alright, Grubby who didn't really like dogs, began to enjoy throwing a ball and racing Pat to pick it up. But on this occasion, as they were running, Pat attacked Grubby's leg. It was a nasty bite and they decided to take the dog back to its kennel and go to the A&E at the local hospital. The doctor checked Grubby's leg and instructed the nurse how it should be dressed and to administer a Tetanus injection in his bottom. Which Grubby didn't like, he yelled a little.

* * *

Two weeks later, Mr Nash was preparing to go out and he decided to take Pat with him. He thought it wise to muzzle Pat as a precaution, just to avoid any problems. He bent down to put the muzzle on Pat's jaw, the dog turned on him, savaging his hand. The attack was so vicious his wife couldn't help so she called the police, they decided to bring a vet, who promptly sedated the dog. It was attacking anyone who came near. Mr Nash's hand was operated on and the operation was successful in saving his fingers.

Chapter 8

The boys had been to the pictures and were walking along the road leading home, when they saw Mr and Mrs Burnley going out for the evening. Grubby looked at Skinner, "Let's go and rattle the front door of the stuck up twins, as they are in alone." They went to the house and hid behind a privet hedge then picked up some pebbles. They threw the small stones at the front door, one of the girls came to the front door to see who was knocking, seeing no one around, and she closed the door. The boys then threw more stones at the door but this time they heard the sound of breaking glass. They both ran away quickly, heading for their own houses.

When Skinner went into his house, his mother looked at him and sensed something was wrong. "What on earth is the matter Ron?"

"Nothing I am going to my bedroom."

"Ron, are you telling me the truth?"

"No"

"We threw stones at the Burnley twin's front door but the stones broke the glass, as you know the doors have small windows at the top half."

"You had better go to your room and I will discuss it with your father and see what he has to say about it. He should be home shortly."

Skinner went upstairs to his bedroom, he knew he was in trouble, he sat on his bed listening for his father to arrive home, when he heard the back door open, he didn't know quite what to do.

Ten minutes later he called Skinner to come downstairs. His father looked up from the paper he was reading.

"Were you alone or was Freddie with you?"

"Yes dad, it was both of us."

"Right, you wait here."

Skinner's father went next door to speak to Freddie's father Sam and told him the story, they both had a good laugh but Sam put a stern look back on his face, turning to Freddie, "Put your coat on and come with me." He insisted the boy went with him.

They took the boys with them to visit Mr Burnley's address. They knocked on the door.

Mr Burnley opened the door. "Hello Sam"

"These two ruffians are here to apologise for breaking your window."

"Come in Sam and Albert, now what is this all about?"

"It appears, these two boys threw stones at your door to annoy the two girls but it went wrong, they broke a small pane of glass on your front door."

Albert stood back, looking at the boys, "What are you going to say?"

"We are sorry Mr Burnley, it won't happen again." They said this together.

Mr Burnley smiled.

"We have brought these two urchins to apologise and they will meet the expense of putting right the damage they have caused. Their month's pocket money will just about pay for the damage." The fathers tried to keep a straight face. "Right Sam, the size of the broken pane is 6 inches square and is frosted glass." The boys were not very comfortable while the conversation was taking place, to make matters even worse, the twin girls could be seen giggling and laughing at the boys' situation.

* * *

The following morning the boys visited a small builder's yard, as they entered the main door, a loud booming voice from the rear of the shop saying, "Can I help you?"

"Yes please, we need a piece of frosted glass 6 inches square and a small amount of putty."

The man came around from his office, he was a tall large gentleman, with a red face and very jovial.

"Don't tell me you have smashed a window, his loud laughter filled the room, his laughter was infectious, the boys joined in with his laughter. Have you the job of replacing the window?"

"Yes mister but we are not too sure how to do it."

* * *

"Right, the first thing is to cut the glass to the correct size, Ah! This should be about the right size" he picked up a piece of glass from a pile, checking the size with his ruler as he said it. "Make sure all the old glass is removed out of the rebate. Put a thin roll of putty in the rebate, push the pane of glass against it, when you are satisfied the new pane is in place, knock a panel pin in the rebate each side, to keep it in position and then put the putty all the way round."

"What is the address where you will be working?"

The boys told him.

"I will be passing there later; I will call to make sure you are okay and making a good job of it." Again, as they were working, the girls were making fun of the boys' situation.

The man from the builder's yard was as good as his word, he did call. He looked at the job; he went to his van and came back with a putty knife. He just wielded the knife around the edge of the rebate, it looked perfect.

"Thank you sir, that does look a really good job now."

"Now, you young gentlemen, to whom shall I send the bill to for the glass and putty, you didn't pay me any money?"

"We will get our pocket money at the end of the week, may we call and pay you then please? We promise, you will be paid."

"If you don't pay me, you will have to work in my shop to clear the debt." They all burst out laughing. "Cheers, for now lads, I look forward to you calling at the week-end." The man really enjoyed dealing with the boys.

Chapter 9

Grubby and Skinner had completed the rebuilding of the two bikes with the help of the man at the back of the cycle shop. Skinner's payment of one nut must have tickled his sense of humour, it still makes the boys smile. The man was called up into the armed forces the following week. They were outside their house on the pavement, polishing their red framed bikes, a neighbour walked up to them. "Are you lads busy?"

"No, Mrs Hester," the boys replied wondering what she was going to say. "My, sister-in-law, has been looking after her husband's pigeon loft, since he was called up into the forces but now she is ill and her doctor forbids her to go outside the warm house. It is two weeks since the inside the loft was cleaned, I have been going down to throw some feed inside the loft but it is too much for me to cope with, will you help?"

"Of course we will Mrs Hester, where does the lady live and what's her name?"

"Her name is Mrs Turner and she lives five minutes from the loft, number two Kingsmead Road."

The boys jumped on their bikes and off they pedalled. They found number two and they went to the back door and knocked. A lady opened the door, "Good morning, are you Mrs. Turner?"

"Yes I am", "Mrs Hester sent us to help you with the pigeon loft."

"Wonderful", "We haven't dealt with pigeons before but we can learn?"

"Mrs Hester suggests we first clean the inside of the loft, as you have been unable to do it yourself, due to your health problem."

"That is so kind of you both, I am unable to pay you at present but I'll make it up to you."

"Don't worry Mrs Turner, we are only too pleased to help."

"There is a cupboard underneath the loft by the door, in there, you will find a tin box, which is the food and the larger box contains scrapers, brushes and a shovel. I will give you the key to the main cupboard, please take care of it,"

"Mrs Hester, we will be very careful".

* * *

The following day, the boys went to attend to the pigeon loft, they were very concerned how the birds were madly fluttering around while they were trying to clean up. They decided to ask Mrs Turner if the birds can be let out. When they did ask Mrs Turner, she immediately said, "Yes, I will come with you, they can be let out to fly and they will return to the loft." When they arrived at the loft, Mrs Turner showed the boys how to open a small door to allow the birds to fly out. The pigeons flew around in a closed bunch for a while and then they settled on to the board at the front of the loft. They pushed the hanging wires to allow them to go inside the loft.

Mrs Turner explained, you can't push the wires open from the inside. When all the birds are in the loft, a small strip of wood is placed across the wires inside to prevent any cats or vermin entering. The boys were fascinated, to see, how the birds shaped their wings like a horse-shoe, as they plummeted down towards the loft.

Looking around the inside of the loft, they could see it was very messy, they set to with the scraper first and when the shed sides and floor were clean, they swept all the droppings into the shovel. They could see where the droppings had been tipped previously, so they piled it on the same compost heap, ready for the allotment people to take. Having cleaned the loft up they went back to Mrs Turner's house telling her that loft had been cleaned and they were off home. "Would you like us to come down and feed the pigeons in the morning? We will be going back to school in two weeks' time, we will have to make other arrangements then."

"If you have time in the morning to pop down and feed the birds, I would be most grateful."

Chapter 10

Skinner went next door to meet up with Grubby and they decided to go out and wander, hoping to come up with some money making scheme. They strolled towards the fields and went under the archway into the large field. They were surprised by the amount of people working away on their allotments. Beyond the allotments, they could see some men building what looked like a timber shed.

They went up to where the men were working and a man was standing by himself, looking at the timber building. "What are you building Mister?"

"You are a nosey young man."

"I am not just nosey Mister. We are always looking out for any little jobs to earn some money."

"Do you live locally?"

"Yes sir, we live in one of the houses, you can see over the bank."

"Would you two boys like the job of cleaning the stables, when they are completed and two horses are installed? Obviously I will pay you, the amount will depend on, if you do a good job and also, a lot is how you get on with the horses. I will show how to put the bit in the horse's mouth and put on the reins. Then walk them around, if you are okay with that, I will get a couple of saddles for you to exercise them properly."

"I must tell you, both horses are very valuable and I have great hopes for them in the coming racing season. So, please take care."

"The bran and hay will be kept in a small shed, which will be built alongside the stables and it will be locked, for which, you will have a key. The man started laughing, you might need to borrow a barn cat from the local farmer, hoping, to keep the mice population under control. You will always find vermin where animal feed is stored. Right lads, I will see you tomorrow morning."

* * *

The boys were so excited, they were at the stables quite early the following morning and they stood about waiting for the horses to arrive. Suddenly they saw a horse box emerge from under the archway into the field and it motored until it was abreast of the stables. The first thing the man did, was to go into the stables and sprinkled sawdust on the floor of the stables and put hay in long troughs in each stable and water in a large bowl. As he led the horses down the tailpiece from the wagon, they looked beautiful, the first one was a dapple Grey and was very docile but the other one was jet black and very lively. He put the bit in the mouth of the grey horse, no trouble at all. When he went to the Black Horse it started prancing about and he got very cross, he could do nothing with the horse. Skinner stepped forward, put his arm around the horse's neck and he appeared to be fondling the animal's ears and speaking to it. The horse stopped jumping about and became very quiet. The man was amazed, he handed the harness and the bit to Skinner and he proceeded to deal with the horse as the boss had dealt with the grey horse. The man and his friends all clapped their hands, to applaud Skinner's actions. Skinner passed the harness over the horses head and walked towards the boss, the horse followed him. When he stopped the horse rested its muzzle on his shoulder. "How! On earth did you do that?"

"I've had experience at my uncle's farm, dealing with obstinate Shire horses, it is the question of gaining the horses trust but allowing the horse to think it is in charge."

Chapter 11

When the snow did arrive, nobody showed any interest in buying or hiring the sledges. They were disappointed but decided to keep the sledges and try to create a sledging craze during the next school holiday. The place they had in mind was the railway bank, which had a very steep fall on the grass bank from the railway line to the bottom of the bank. This would be an ideal sledge run, next to a brick archway.

The boys decided to go to the top of the bank to check it was completely safe as a tall wire fence had been erected to prevent anyone getting on to the railway line. There was a small brick wall built along the top of the archway and this is where the boys could hide. While they were checking, a vehicle came up the road and parked under the arch, Grubby being an avid number taker, he entered the numbers of the plate in his book. They got well down below the top of the wall away from sight, as they were on private land.

A lot of activity was being carried out below; obviously a mechanical repair was being carried out to the van. Suddenly the engine started up and the van reversed out of the archway. Grubby quickly said "That is not the number plate on the van when it went under the arch." Arriving home, Skinner told his father about the van changing its number plate, Grubby has the number when it arrived and when it left.

"Have you told the police?"

"No, the last time we reported a break-in, they laughed at us and told us to go home."

"Sam and I are going to the local for a darts match this evening, we will go with you to the police station, it is on our way."

When they called at the police station Sam briefly told the sergeant about the changing of the number plates.

"Have you the new numbers?" Grubby gave him a copy of the original plates and the numbers of the new plate.

The sergeant burst out laughing, "Thank you, thank you very much. This van was stolen and we now know why it couldn't be traced. The van was loaded with very valuable furniture, with material to build a platform and all the props that were going to be used when they arrived at Earls Court. They planned to display their goods at the furniture exhibition. As you know, the exhibition is the highlight of the furniture year and the competition is great, hoping to obtain orders from warehouses and stores."

They learned later that the van had been traced to Scotland, they were not sure, if the furniture was to be sold there or if was going to be shipped abroad. Either way, the factory owner was delighted with the outcome.

The driver and his mate were arrested but they absconded whilst waiting for a translator, they denied any knowledge of the English language.

* * *

There was excitement in the air because Fairground Engines were seen pulling into a large field. All the local children went hoping to get a job which would lead to a free ride, when all the amusements were set up. This was the normal practice, when the fair was all set up and ready to open. The man in charge would blow a whistle and wave his arms and all the children would come running and jump on the roundabout, each selecting one of the brightly painted horses, for the free ride on the Carousel.

After going home to have their tea they decided to visit the fair again. The coloured lights with the fairground organ playing created a magical atmosphere but as the dusk crept in, all the lights would be extinguished to conform to the Blackout Regulations. Skinner could not understand how several of the musical notes sounded peculiar, in fact, he could hear a separate beat in the background and the beat somehow sounded like the Morse code, as the man at the Cadets had instructed.

He called to Grubby. "I know you regard me as a hair brain but I want you to join me and concentrate on what I am saying. Listen to the music carefully, there are some particular notes played and the beat in the background sounds like Morse code." Grubby listened, "Yes it does sound like a code."

"I'll nip home and get my notebook and the card."

Grubby came tearing back, waving his book and pencil in the air.

They both stood listening to the music and eventually they agreed on B4A6, W22B and B8AZ. "Do you think it is anything important Grubby?"

"I'm not sure, let us go to the Police Station and show it to them."

They entered the Police Station and the officer at the desk said. "Right boys, can I help you?"

"The boys explained about the background beat to the fairground organ music and the message they have picked up from it."

"Let me read it" After reading the numbers, he just laughed. "What boys' magazine are you reading?" He handed the piece of paper back to Skinner, "Off you go boys."

"What shall we do now Grubby?"

"I know, let us take it to the cadet officer, he will tell us if it is just nonsense or not."

They went to the officer's house and he was very surprised to see them on his doorstep. Before he could say anything, Skinner said, "Please don't laugh at us as the policeman did." They explained about the beat in the music and how it relates to these numbers using this, holding up the Morse card. He looked at the numbers, "They look like co-ordinates on a map or chart. Write your addresses on the back of this piece of paper and I will look into it for you. You were quite right to bring these numbers to my attention. I will make a few enquiries and I will come back to you. Give me a copy of the numbers."

"Come along Grubby, my mother will grumble, you are staying with me for your tea and we are late." They both started running laughing and giggling. Grubby was right, his mother did grumble at them for being late but she still smiled at the boys. They were just finishing their cup of tea, when Grubby's sister said "There is a big black limousine pulling up on our front drive and two men in officer's uniform getting out."

They all jumped when there was a loud knocking on the front door, Grubby's mother looked at the boys, "What! Have you two been up to now?"

She went to the front door, when she opened it she was taken aback. Standing on the doorstep were two tall men in uniform, one had several wavy golden stripes round the cuff of his uniform and the other had three gold bands. The taller of the two said, "Mrs Wharton?"

"Yes, can I help you?"

" I would like to speak to two boys nicknamed Grubby and Skinner, are they here?"

"Yes, what have they been up to now?"

"They have done nothing wrong but I am hoping they can help me."

"You had better come in."

The two boys were cowering behind the kitchen door.

"Come along boys, these gentlemen would like to speak to you."

They crept into the lounge looking very sheepish.

"We had a phone call from your cadet officer, will you show me the numbers you took from the organ music, please?"

Grubby got his notebook out and passed it to the officer, they looked at the book. One of the men went outside to his car and he came back with a long cylindrical looking object, from which, he took out a large chart, "May I lay the chart on the table Mrs

Wharton?" The boys were looking over his shoulder and saw it was a chart of the Atlantic Ocean. "Good Lord, These coordinates are exactly where the convoys are meeting up tomorrow night. Someone is passing this information on to enable a pack of U-Boats to plan a reception committee. This convoy is bringing armament's and most important, food for the tables of this country. May I use your phone?"

He came back saying, "I have reversed the charge of the phone call, Mrs Wharton."

"Will you all sit down please, what you have just witnessed is strictly confidential and I don't want you to discuss it with anyone, obviously you will tell your husband but please keep this between ourselves. These boys have been very clever, they could have saved the lives of a hundred or more sailors by finding this information. We must keep quiet about this, while we investigate the organ music. We must go now, if you pick up any different messages ring this number. Just dial the phone number and read out the number on this card and you will be put straight through and the call will cost nothing." When the officers had gone, Grubby's mum looked at the boys saying "Well I never," Bertha often used that expression but the family never knew what she meant by it, or even what it is supposed to mean.

Chapter 12

The boys were walking around the field near the railway bridge, when suddenly the deafening roar of an aircraft engine filled the air. Looking up they saw a German aircraft plummeting down towards them. They were terrified, they threw themselves on to the ground thinking the plane would hit them. When they raised their heads, they could see the aircraft had crash landed a few hundred yards from them. They automatically ran to the plane and they could see the pilot struggling to get out. A small flame was licking around the engine. They quickly wrestled the twisted canopy off to enable the pilot to get out of the aircraft. As he jumped on to the ground, he grabbed the boys making them run away from the plane, they were just a few yards away, the aircraft exploded.

When they picked themselves up, the pilot was facing them pointing a gun at them, neither Grubby or Skinner realised the seriousness of the situation, they started laughing. The pilot became unsure of himself, he too started laughing and threw the gun away. Skinner shouted, "Come" and the three of them went to Skinner's house. When they arrived at his house, his mother was quite nervous but when the pilot removed his leather helmet, they were all surprised. He was a very young boy, about the same age as her own son. With him being so young, May warmed to him, thinking his mother will wonder where he is. Dead, Alive or a Prisoner of War?

The pilot had several wounds to his face and he was holding his shoulder, as if in pain. May asked Bertha to come into her house and attend to the young boy but first, she organised a hot bath for him. When he had bathed and dried himself, Bertha attended to his head wounds. Bertha had been a nurse in her younger days and the neighbours always turned to her, when in need of medical attention.

The pilot answered to the name Fritz, so that is what they called him. He was so unsure of himself, the enemy were nothing like, what he had been led to believe. Bertha finished dressing the boys' wounds and they all sat down at the tea table to enjoy a meal. It was during the meal an ARP man called, asking if they had seen the pilot of the crashed aircraft. He was amazed when he was introduced to the young boy. "You realise the army will call for him?"

"Surely he can stay here a while?"

"I doubt it." As they were talking an army truck pulled up outside the house. An army officer got out and came to the door. "We called for the pilot of the crashed aircraft, whom I understand is here."

The boy had finished his meal, he got up and shook hands with Grubby and Skinner and he hugged May and Bertha with tears in his eyes. He was then marched away between two soldiers, each carrying a rifle with fixed bayonets. They were sorry to see him go.

Chapter 13

Bertha was surprised to have a parcel delivered addressed to her. When she opened the parcel she found two smaller parcels addressed to the two boys. They were addressed to Grubby and Skinner. She took Skinner's parcel next door to May, Skinner's mother. May, was tempted to unwrap the parcel but she waited until her son came home. When the boys arrived home, they both ran into Skinner's house. His mother handed him the parcel, he ripped the paper off and was delighted, and it was a black leather note book and a fountain pen. On the centre of the front cover, was the Royal Naval emblem with Royal Navy written in gold lettering curved round the emblem, most impressive. Grubby went dashing home, hoping he had a parcel, he ripped the wrapping off and he was delighted to find he had the same as Skinner. When his mother was folding up the wrapping paper a card fell out, it was from Admiral Marks saying: "Thank you boys for saving many lives." Both boys puffed out their chests and strutted around trying to look important.

Several days later they had a visit from another Royal Navy Officer. He asked the boys to visit the fairground and carefully listen to the music, try to pick out the letters and numbers as before, if you can. Make a note of them and I will call later this week. We are most grateful to you boys but do be careful not make it look too obvious what you are doing, many thanks, he said good night to Mrs Wharton and left the house.

The boys decided to go out and wander round the fairground, as before, the different coloured fairy lights still made the area look magical to the boys. They wandered around listening to the organ music very carefully. Then suddenly they looked at each other and smiled, they listened to what they thought they were looking for and they wrote it down in their books. They decided to go home and compare notes and luckily they had both come up with the same numbers and letters.

Two nights later the RN Officer called asking if they had been successful? When they showed the officer the signal they had picked up, he became excited, by this time he had been joined by another officer. They got up to leave saying how grateful they were for the boys' efforts but pleaded with them to keep all this under their hats.

The boys learned at a later date, what they had been asked to check was the message the boffins in the Admiralty had planted and it had been transmitted correctly; hopefully the spy will have picked it up. The coordinates contained in that message, indicated, where a convoy of thirty merchant ships would be on the day and time shown in the message. A pack of German U Boats had converged on the coordinates planning to ambush the convoy but instead of a convoy of merchant ships arriving, it was a flotilla of RN Destroyers designed to hunt submarines. The result was four submarines were captured and three were destroyed when fleeing from the destroyers.

* * *

Fate intervened and a strange twist to life, Skinner married Mary one of the Burnley twins and strange as it might seem, Grubby married her twin, Rose. So, they were both married before they went off into the Navy. The girl's father was pleased that they had a double wedding, bearing in mind the cost. All the neighbours chipped in to make the wedding a success for which the parents were delighted; the food and clothing were strictly rationed and the neighbours help was appreciated. It helped to make it a happy day for the boys and their wives. The parting of the ways came sooner than the boys had hoped, Grubby received his calling up papers to join the Royal Navy some two months before Skinner. They both trained as a Telegraphist, Grubby in Portsmouth and Skinner in Dundee.

The Telegraphist course, stretched to eighteen weeks and when they had completed the eighteen weeks course, they could read a message at eighteen words a minute. Grubby served on a MTB, Motor Torpedo Boat, and Skinner on a Destroyer. Sadly Grubby was killed in action. He had been home on a week-end leave, the weekend prior to his death. He was given a pass and travel voucher, because the engines on his MTB had developed a fault, it was decided to give the engine a complete overhaul during the weekend. When he returned to his depot from his leave, the depot was in a panic, it was rumoured that two German Warships would be sailing down the English Channel. The rumour turned out to be correct. The MTBs were ordered to sea and Grubby's Captain spotted one of the warships and he ordered an attack. They began their attacking run to fire a torpedo. As they approached to launch the torpedo, their engine stopped and they became stationery, a dead duck on the sea. The crew on the German warship started firing on them and the Skipper decided to abandon the MTB and get in to a Carly Float Dinghy. The enemy gunner started firing machine gun bullets round the float in a circle and he gradually reduced the circle killing all but one of the occupants on the float, the survivor was badly injured.

The bodies and the badly injured man were brought back to the base, sad, that is the story as told by the survivor. Grubby's body was brought home and buried in his local cemetery.

* * *

Even many years later when Skinner had been demobbed, married to Mary with a family. His wife would find him, sitting looking into the fire laughing and still arguing with his pal Grubby. One day he will tell his boys of the antics Grubby and he got up to, hoping they will not get in the same tangles as they did. It was great fun.

Rose, Grubby's wife, walked across to a side window of their house and what she saw brought a lump in her throat, she saw her son Paul and Skinners son John, run across to the playing fields, clutching a football. Thinking, I wonder if they are referred to as Grubby and Skinner by their friends. I really do hope they will get as much excitement out of their boyhood life as their fathers did. I am surprised their fathers didn't get locked up by P.C Mathews.

* * *

Mary stood, still looking out of the window reminiscing, the two boys came dashing through the back door. They went straight to Ron's father, "Will you tell us how to get little jobs, to help with our pocket money, as you and my dad used to?"

"Now that is a tall order, there are so many jobs you could do. Let me think about it."

"You could run errands, gardening, dog walking and chopping firewood, there are numerous odd jobs you could do to make money."

"Don't tell me! You are going to be "Young Grubby and Young Skinner?" Laughing, Freddie said, "That's a good one, Young Skinner."

Skinner sat thinking about his and Fred's escapades in years gone by, how did we get away with some of our dodges. The boys' jobs must be more straight forward than the ones we did and more legal. He couldn't help smiling when he thought back to their escapades and what fun they had. Give me a few days to think about it and I will tell you how and what to do and keep out of trouble.

Chapter 14

Thinking back, Skinner's memory drifted to when he joined a brand new Destroyer in Barrow-in-Furness. Having arrived on a troop train from Devonport Barracks, the train contained the whole ships company.

Having all the ratings settled down into their various mess-decks, the serious work began and each member found out with whom they would be working over the months to come and which of the senior officers they would be answerable to during any operation.

The ship and the crew, will be subjected to any eventuality, each faced during the coming weeks, before the ship is ready to face the enemy. The trials that are to take place are referred to as the working up trials, which, are supposed to get the ship, the crew and any sophisticated instruments the crew are expected to work with, to be completely at one.

* * *

After all the working up trials had been completed, the Ship builders officially handed the vessel over to the Admiralty Department. The first given duty, was to escort a Submarine from its mooring basin, to the open seas. A Submarine sailing on the surface was always very vulnerable, to an enemy air attack. When the Submarine had submerged below the surface of the sea, the escort returned back to its mooring.

Two days later, Skinners destroyer set sail to join up with two other destroyers, to act as escort, or as some wags would refer to the job as a "Mother Hen" to two Aircraft Carriers. The operation entailed the bombing a German Pocket Battleship, named TIRPITZ, which was holed up in a Norwegian fjord. The reason it was there, was to have its steering gear repaired. An allied aircraft had caught it on the open seas and carried out an attack, with some success. The defences and build of this vessel, was the envy of all ship designers, it was a small, compact but a very powerful ship.

The raid on the Tirpitz went off exactly as had been planned. The whole operation was built and planned, on information supplied by our own secret agents on site.

The homeward journey was reasonably quiet; there were several air raid alerts but not enough to have some of the watch keepers to lose sleep.

While on watch in the radio room, Skinner received a message which he immediately passed to the Skipper on the bridge. The message was advising that a German Midget Submarine had penetrated the defences into Scapa Flow, much to the dismay of the authorities. The last time this happened, a British Battleship was sunk with a great loss of life. Arriving back at the Flow, the senior skipper, decided to give orders to roll off several depth charges from the stern, set at various depths, hoping to force the enemy to the surface.

This did not produce the answer the skipper had hoped for. The other ships entered the Flow but they were all told to "Drop Anchor and stop engines, to enable their instruments, to do an underwater sweep.

The first Lieutenant took up his position on the Forecastle, watching for the Skipper to indicate the order for the Anchor to be dropped.

The Skipper raised his arm, lowering to indicate drop anchor, shouting "LET GO." A rating, used a hammer to remove the block securing the anchor chain. The anchor slid silently down into the sea, as it reached the sea bottom, the Captain ordered slow astern to grapple the anchor on the sea bed.

It was a few minutes before it was realised, that the rating on the stern had reacted to "LET GO" and had rolled a depth charge over the stern into the sea. When it was realised, the depth charge was beneath the ship about amidships. The explosion was very powerful and it caused serious structural damage to the vessel, a floating dock was rushed out to prevent any possibility of the

Destroyer sinking. The sad part of the accident was it caused the death of six ratings. The ship could be repaired.

Chapter 15

The following morning the ship's crew were all lined up to hear a message from the ship's captain. The ship is being decommissioned, you will all be given a seven day leave, at the end of your leave, you will return to your depot. I would think most of you will be returning to Devonport Barracks, as this ship is a Devonport vessel.

I must express my sorrow, having lost six of our shipmates in the accident yesterday, we will all be attending the funeral ashore in Lyness. After which, the railway passes and your leave passes will be ready for you.

After the funeral, they all lined up to receive the passes, as had been arranged and transport was laid on to take them to the railway station, each going their different ways.

Skinner's parents were delighted when he arrived home, they had no word from him for two weeks previously and they had become concerned, especially as the "Lord Haw-Haw" broadcast, had said "Skinner's ship had been destroyed by their wonderful submarine crews." The seven days leave were thoroughly appreciated but it went by far too quickly. His mother was in tears as the good-byes were said and Skinner set off on his journey to Devonport Barracks.

Reporting back to the barracks, he was given a space to hang his hammock and a cupboard to put his belongings in. The following day, his name was called out on the Tannoy system, telling him to report to the regulating office. There, he was given a railway pass, to cover his journey to Lowestoft which is the Patrol Service depot. He started his journey after lunch. He was taken to the railway station, helped with his kitbag and his hammock but he clutched his small suitcase.

The journey, took a long time due to the hold ups with air raids and cancelled trains, mainly due to troop movements. Skinner eventually arrived at Lowestoft in the early hours of the morning, needless to say, there was not a soul about. He spotted a policeman, "May I sleep in one of yours cells tonight please?"

"Sorry lad, the cells are all full up tonight with drunks, Come with me."

The Policeman took him to the Salvation Army Reception House. On arrival, a lady popped her head above the counter. "Yes young man, can we help you?" The policeman explained, "this young man had just arrived on the last train and he has nowhere to sleep, also he tells me he only has two pence."

The lady just smiled, "Have you eaten"?

"No, not since my breakfast this morning."

"Come with me." In about five minutes Skinner was faced with a plate of sausage, beans, toast and of course, the usual cup of tea.

He was taken to a small cubicle, which contained a bed and a nearby toilet. He was advised to sleep on his money belt and his boots, "just in case" said she smiling.

He had a good night's sleep and a breakfast was ready for him, when went to the desk to thank them. They knew he had no money to contribute and they just waived away any apologies for not paying. From that day on, he has never turned his back on the Salvation Army collecting boxes.

He went to the dockyard, to report to his ship. He was astounded when he saw his next berth. It was an all wooden ship. Referred to as a MMS Class Ship known as a Motor Mine Sweeper. It was 112 feet in length and had a 21 foot beam; one wonders how it would fair in a storm. It being double LL minesweeper, it towed a long double cable which pulsated, sending out electric negative waves and then positive waves, hoping to explode magnetic mines within its range, still that is another story. These little ships were referred to as MICKEY MOUSE SHIPS, Double LL Sweepers. Apart from all the jokes, it was very efficient machine and it carried out the job, it was made to do.

Skinner went on board, not forgetting to salute the ensign, waving in the breeze at the stern. He reported to the cox-swain, known to the crew as the cox, who then took him down forward to show him his mess. He was told he would be sharing the mess with wireman, signalman and coder. The man who introduced himself as the wireman, said, he deals with the electric cables that are run out to activate and explode the mines. The beds are on hinges, to enable them to be pushed up against the ships side when not in use and the seating will lift, to put any clothing in a small area like a cupboard. No matter when you joined new ship, one of the first questions was "Are you Grog or Temperance or UA?" Do you take your ration of Rum or are you under age? Which was so, in my case. Just.

Chapter 16

When Skinner saw members of the crew, getting ready to go ashore, he noticed that several of them had a small replica of a metal mine, sewn on the cuff of his uniform. When he asked, one of the men just smiled, "The life expectancy on these minesweepers is six months. If, I say if, you survive that length of time, you can apply for a badge."

The smile, would be wiped off the following day. After completing the days sweeping pattern, the signal flags went up to "In sweeps". It was the leading ship who set the pace, all the crew divided and went to the handle each side of the drum to wind in the cables, there was always a lot of competition to see which ship could get the sweep in the fastest. Even cigarettes were sometimes gambled on the outcome.

As the sweeps were being wound in, a mine must have come adrift from a rusted cable on the seabed due to the bad weather; it had risen to the surface and it got tangled with the cable. When the mine hit the stern, it exploded, destroying the vessel and the life on board.

Tragedy struck again that afternoon, an Allied aircraft, jettisoned his bombs into the sea, due to the aircraft being badly damaged. The bombs landed on a minesweeper, again destroying the ship and its crew.

A Wren on duty in the control room, had tears in her eyes as she removed the numbered sweeper from the board, knowing she would not meet her boyfriend at the local dance that evening.

The commander in charge of keeping the lanes swept for mines, was getting a little disturbed, he was losing craft but was unable to obtain replacements. A convoy was due in a few days and he was still responsible for keeping the lanes mine free.

There had been another problem to contend with. The enemy had introduced an acoustic mine that would explode reacting to the ship's engine noise as it passed over the mine. The enemy had also perfected a way of making it explode, not on the first, second and so on, but regulated to explode on any one ship, whether it may be number one or number five; a lottery on the number. This certainly created a problem for the convoys. This is another problem, for the backroom boys to find the answer to, before, a heavy loss of life.

* * *

The ship that Skinner was on, was called into the dockyard and an angled frame fitted on each side of the bow of the ship, the frame could be lifted in or out of the sea using a cable. The tip that enters the sea held a big drum and the noise it made, was the same as a pneumatic drill, used the dig up a roadway. On the trial, It exploded an acoustic mine. This system was fitted to all the small minesweepers with great success and it overcame the lottery of under which ship would the mine explode. The noise was very uncomfortable throughout the ship, because of its musical beat. Even that, was better than spending a night, in the cold of an open boat, hoping against hope, to be picked up the following day.

* * *

A message was received, instructing the captain to proceed to the Portsmouth dockyard. Neither, the skipper, nor the officers had any idea why. They arrived to their destination, in the early hours of the morning On arrival they were directed to the quayside mooring area.

The first thing the following morning, several dockyard engineers boarded the ship and started fitting a winch on the forward and aft decks. The next happening was, the workmen started feeding a strong cable on to the winches. In spite of questioning the engineers, they could not provide the answers, as to what the cables were going to be used for.

They were all astounded, when two barrage balloons were brought on board and attached to the cable ends. Having secured everything safely, they set sail, the destination was unknown. Gradually, it became clear, as they approached the Normandy coast and the balloons were allowed to rise in the sky. There were several small minesweepers like ourselves, lined up all with balloons. At daybreak we saw several large Battleships arriving.

* * *

In position, they started firing over the balloons, pounding the French beach and the enemy's gun emplacements. The balloons were there, to stop enemy aircraft diving down and attacking the Battleships. To this day, anyone who experienced the terrifying scream as a Stuka Aircraft dived to attack them, would cringe, when they heard a similar noise by a lorry or a bus. The noise was generated via fins that had been fitted to create this noise as the wind passed through them. For them the fear was always there.

One hour later we saw landing craft loaded with soldiers and tanks approaching the beach and then we realised, it was the start, of a planned operation. The long awaited invasion, to regain control of the countries occupied by the enemy.

* * *

Skinner, was watching and wondering about the outcome. What a waste of lives but unfortunately, necessary for the future of Europe.

The minesweepers, which, had the Barrage Balloons anchored to a cable on board, were instructed to close up to the invasion craft. Hopefully, to prevent the enemy aircraft from strafing them with machine or cannon fire and killing the invading forces before they land on the beaches. The invading troops landed and due to speed they advanced quickly. Supplies became a worry to the Army chiefs, food being the biggest problem. A meeting was held and it was decided to use the Sea Basins in Le Havre where the transporting ships could use the Basins to be unloaded. Smaller vessels could then be used to transport the goods down the River Seine to be collected by the various units. Food was always the biggest problem.

Chapter 17

Three of the minesweepers were sent off to ensure the Basins were clear of any booby traps or any explosives lurking below the surface. On arrival a small boat was used to drag the LL cable around the surface of the sea in the basin. When the cables were in place, the cables were activated, hoping to explode any Magnetic Mines but there was no response. The next step was to use hand grenades thrown into the water at different intervals and counting to allow for the various depths, again hoping to explode any acoustic mines below the surface, which, could have been left as a trap. Two days of grenade explosions and activated magnetic cables, the Basins were now regarded as safe to accept transport vessels. The officers in charge of the advancing troops, breathed a sigh of relief.

The sweepers left there and proceeded down the River Seine, the skipper decided to moor up opposite two American Liberty Ships.

Early the following morning at 4 am, a loud explosion awakened most of the ship's crew. It was obvious the enemy had changed its tactics. On checking, it was found the enemy had created a floating bomb, the base was like a large football and it had a vertical centre post, from the centre post were umbrellas splines. When the splines came into contact with a stationary object, it would activate an explosion. These bombs were being floated down the river, to destroy the temporary bridges across the River Seine that the Royal Engineers had erected.

During the morning Skinners Captain was alerted, the crew of the Liberty were being marched off the ship; ashore, one of the crew pointed out why. There was a floating bomb bouncing against the hull of the ship. The Captain said, "Lower the small boat", no one was happy about going on the small boat. The captain pointed. "You, you and you come with me" They had no option, they got into the boat with the captain. "Lower away."

The man on the tiller took the boat alongside the Liberty Ship. The Skipper leaned over the side on the boat, picked up the floating bomb, holding the centre post very carefully, keeping away from the splines, which, would explode the bomb. He then held it very carefully away from himself while the tiller man guided the boat ashore. The Skipper stood the bomb on the bank, and the bomb disposable people would come along and defuse it.

There came very loud cheering, from the Liberty ship.

The officers of the advancing troops began to get very concerned, the floating bomb was having a devastating effect on the stocks of food and ammunition.

The enemy was targeting the bridges, using the floating bombs, which was playing havoc with the road transport.

* * *

The Skipper and his officers were invited for drinks aboard the Liberty Ship, he accepted and he brought his ship alongside. While they were having drinks the crew were given bars of nut milk chocolate, cigars and packets of silk stockings. For whom they were intended, no mention was made.

The telegraphist from the Liberty ship joined Skinner in his radio room. Skinner produced a bottle of rum which he had filled by putting part of his ration each day, this was strictly forbidden but there were ways. They talked about their families at home, when Skinner mentioned that he had a sister, he popped off and came back with another packet of silk stockings. "Thank you very much."

"Not at all. We don't want Mother and daughter falling out over stockings," laughing as he said it.

They both set to, devouring the bottle rum.

A high level meeting was arranged and the Captains from the three sweepers were asked to attend. There were several ideas thrown around, hoping to find the answer to their problem.

Skinner's, Skipper chipped in, "May I make a suggestion? Our sweepers have a very shallow draught, if each of the sweepers is loaded with an amount of food and supplies, we could use the smaller rivers and get the goods to the troops, where they are badly needed. We would have two smaller boats go on ahead to either explode or defuse any floating mines."

The senior General present, looked at the Skipper making the suggestion. "It would be wonderful, if you could manage to deliver the goods. You are aware the enemy will try to prevent such an operation. You must realise, that you are putting your ship and its crew in great danger."

"That is so, but we must try and prevent our troops, from being starved of food and short of ammunition."

"That is a wonderful statement sir, yes, we will try out your suggestion. You will be given our fullest cooperation, whatever you need, just ask."

"Can you arrange a certain amount of Air Cover?"

"I will try but the RAF is very stretched, with the protection of our towns and cities, which, are being targeted. That is one thing that is out of my jurisdiction, but I will try."

* * *

Three sweepers were sent off to Le Havre, to get loaded as planned. Great attention was paid to the amount loaded on each vessel, to ensure the vessel still had a shallow draught. Having loaded, the sweepers set off early the following morning. Skinner's skipper being senior, he led the way. They were very pleased with the amount of distance they had covered but later that day an enemy spotting plane was seen, obviously reporting back any movement. Just as expected, some ten minutes later a Stuka aircraft was seen making towards the sweepers. The Stuka started to dive towards the ships, some of the crew who had experienced this aircraft attack before, waited for a terrifying scream to fill the air.

The members of the crew who not experienced this situation before, their faces went white and in some cases started trembling. It was impossible to describe, the affect the scream had on each of the individual members of the crew. The aircraft raked the sweepers with gunfire, fortunately, no member of the crew was injured, nor was there any damage to the supplies being carried. The skippers of the three vessels breathed a deep sigh of relief.

* * *

The next object was to find a navigational river, nearest to where the troops were located. The charts showing the rivers had been corrupted by the enemy. They took a river which looked reasonable in depth for the ships to travel and the small boats ahead had a very busy time, dealing with the floating bombs and little explosive traps. It became obvious the enemy knew we were trying to keep up with food and supplies for our fast advancing troops.

As the food supplies and ammunition were unloaded from the sweepers, the senior officers felt as if a dark cloud had been lifted. The food and ammunition was what they had hoped for.

Skinner received a message, for which the crew on board cheered out loud. The Admiralty had decided, the crew will also share the decoration, of the France and Germany Medal. The cheering was not as loud and prolonged as when it came over the speaker "Splice the main brace." The crew started rubbing their hands, Rum time, was in one hour. It was planned that sweepers would remain in port for a few days. NOT! I might add, due to the double ration of rum.

Chapter 18

The Admiral and his team became very concerned. The enemies E-Boats were spinning around the Needles area during the night, which was the route the large convoy would be taking when approaching their ports for unloading. He kept looking through his very powerful binoculars, in the direction of the large convoy. He estimated that they were about 15 miles off the coastline. It was possible to see two ships nursing the badly damaged ship, attempting to keep it afloat; this ship was carrying valuable grain from Canada. It was decided to send out two tugs, to assist in bringing the badly damaged ship to the unloading bay. The tugs set off, about two miles from their mooring, one of the tugs exploded, destroying the vessel and the crew on board. The Admiral signalled, for the convoy to remain outside the Needle area and the minefield will be dealt with.

Skinner was on watch in his radio cabin, when he received a message marked "Top Priority", which, he immediately passed to his Captain. The captain smiled, this will upset a lot of my crew, who think they will be going ashore tonight. The watch going ashore were lined up, ready for duty officer to inspect them, before being allowed to go. The captain walked out of his cabin, he shouted, "Stop! Go back to you mess decks and get changed into your seagoing outfits. We are sailing, with the tide in about forty minutes." There was much moaning and groaning but they all did as they were told. Everyone did exactly as they were told, if told to jump, they would ask how high? Such was the discipline.

Three mine sweepers, set off from their mooring on the Seine, heading back to the Needles. The daylight was beginning to turn to dusk but they still had to go as instructed and they knew it would be in the early morning, when they arrived at their destination. On arrival, the captains of each sweeper, were called on board the Admirals ship, he explained how the E-Boats had laid mines, what sort of mines he wasn't sure but unfortunately one of our tugs was destroyed by one.

* * *

On arrival to the area thought to be the mined zone, three sweepers set sail three abreast and swept from the convoy to the unloading area; they swept several times exploding two acoustic and three magnetic mines. The sweepers indicated the cleaned corridor with cones, anchored to the sea bed. This took a whole day; it was decided, to keep the three sweepers abreast and lead the convoy into the port. One officer was heard to say, "A belt and braces job." Once in the port, the tugs would take them to their unloading bays.

The whole operation went off without a hitch, much to the delight of the Admiral and the crews. In fact, the crews have had a torturous journey. The convoy had had packs of U-Boats hunting them and many attacks from the air; they had also lost one ship. The crew had found it most disturbing, seeing their pals being killed and there was so little they could do to help. They thought, they personally, had been very lucky to arrive in port all in one piece. They couldn't wait to get ashore and visit the local Public House to enjoy a pint of beer, which at times during the trip, they thought they would never visit and enjoy again.

The cranes started unloading the ships straight away. The one problem encountered was with unloading the grain into the Silos. The recent air attack, had targeted the docks and the pipes used to transfer the grain had been damaged, so there was a long delay to put things right. As the Admiral said, "That is no problem, now we have the ship alongside."

The large silo was a metal tank, buried and encased in a complete jacket of a thick concrete to safeguard its contents. The clever engineers had installed air conditioning to prevent the grain from going mouldy, much to Lord Woolton's delight. Feeding the country was a constant headache for him; it was his responsibility as the Minister of Food and he did a good job, under very difficult circumstances.

Chapter 19

The rumour flying around the dock yard was the war was coming to a close; how the rumour started, no one knows. The following day an announcement was made, stating the following: "Germany has unconditionally surrendered." Within no time at all, the ships were all flying colourful flags and there was a lot of claxon noise.

The hard work will start quickly. The minefields of the enemies must be cleared and the Allies minefields and the metal anti-Submarine nets would need sorting urgently.

With the announcement that the war had come to an end, the whole country appeared to go mad. Street parties were arranged in fact, any excuse to celebrate, was there.

* * *

The next rumour that flew around was how soon the service men would be able to get back to their homes. This would be after completing the tasks of clearing the nasty mines, booby traps and dangerous bombs that were lying around. They were sent back to their depots and Skinner's Captain told his crew to take all their personal possessions off the ship, as it will be steamed up on the beach and left. The Coxswain and one member of the crew will be on board, when this takes place. The ship was beached and a tractor, dragged it further up the beach, the Coxswain looked at the number of the minesweepers marooned on the beach, he thought it sad. It looked like a graveyard for the many ships, some could tell happy tales and others very sad stories. When this had taken place, they were transported back to their depots, the next step, would be the following day.

* * *

Having arrived back to Devonport, they were sent to various rooms in the barracks, but the place was overcrowded.

There were many ratings in the room allocated to sleep in that small area; there were not any rails to hang their hammocks and they had to unroll the hammock on the floor. The ratings slept on any personal possessions and money belts, rather than lose them.

The following morning, after breakfast, they were marched in an orderly fashion to a large clothing store, as they walked into the store, they were asked size of suit and clothing. Before putting down the size on to paper, one man weighed up their sizes. Stepping along, they were given a suit and other civilian garments. At the end of the long counter, a man checked to ensure they had everything available. They were given a strong brown paper bag, with a strong string at the top of the bag and all the clothes were placed into it. From there they were taken to an office and asked their Pay Roll number; having given that number, they were given a Railway Warrant to the nearest Railway Station to their home.

Having collected all the baggage, they were transported to the local Railway Station. The times of the trains had been noted and they were all put on the correct train.

Skinner arrived at his local station early evening and he splashed out and took a taxi to his home. There was great excitement arriving home, not worrying about when he has to go back to the ship. Skinner looked around and wondered "What was the war all about?" One evening he went to his cupboard and got two bottles of beer out, hesitating, he put one back. His wife smiled, sighed silently, the second bottle was for Grubby. He took his bottle with him to the back of the wood shed which is where he used to sit with Grubby discussing their families, or if they were not at one with their wives.

Taking the top off his bottle of beer, he sipped it and his mind started to wander. He sat talking to his pal Grubby, "I hope our boys get as much fun out of life as we did as youngsters", in his mind, he went through the scrapes they encountered and how they got out of them. This brought a big grin across his face.

Raising his bottle he said "Cheers Pal, we might meet again. WHO Knows?"